GRATEFUL AND BLESSED

Poems

ANCA IVANENKO

Includes the poems published in
"Love by Design, Forgiveness by Choice"

Grateful and Blessed
Copyright © 2022 by Anca Ivanenko

Tellwell Talent
www.tellwell.ca

ISBN
978-0-2288-7406-5 (Paperback)

Table of Contents

To those who love,
To those who suffer,
To those who forgive,
To those who pray…

Until we meet again

To my father

His mind was home to screams of terror—ones nobody could hear.
For him—and with him—life was angst, disappointment and fear.
Trapped in his thoughts, in bars of steel, he lived life as a game,
With no regard for those who loved him, who bore his cross and shame.

He didn't know that he had power. How big he could have been!
He played his life to make a statement; he paid the cost, to win.
To live his way —was his objective—by rules that he enjoys!
Others would beg and scream and summon; all that he heard was noise.

Why would he listen if they pushed him?
Why would he join their world?
Best of intentions made no difference—he heard "rejected", "sold".
Who he was being was a victim; who he was made, was wrong;
And all throughout his time spent living, who he was not, was strong.

In retrospect, he asked for little: he wanted to be free;
He wanted others to accept him, support him, let him be;
He wanted people to acknowledge the things that he held dear
And for the world to know his story, his pain, his voice to hear.

He wanted to be known as proud—never told what to do!
He told the world that he had chosen, and to him, that was true.
It was his choice that *took* his choices, and life. He chose a threat!
Now that he's gone, we light a candle, in honor, and regret.

We honor him for all he suffered, all he gave, all he was;
All his successes and his failures, his greatness and his flaws.
And in the silence of acceptance, we let go of the strain
And send him love, to light his journey, until we meet again.

Two worlds

The world of his: exclusive;
A box where the new will subside;

Where rules are predetermined,
Existing is succeeding,
A world of tradition and pride.

The world of hers: in progress;
A world she creates by design;

In which love conquers reason,
Being equates perception,
Emotion and vision align.

He, to her world, is magic!
Around him, she shines like a jewel!

To his, she is too different;
Two hearts that beat in rhythm;
To love him, is her only rule.

So gracefully defined, subtle and free,
Your hug feels like a breeze, gentle and light.
To all my senses, you are pure delight!
An overwhelming love, that lets me be.

So sensibly refined, soft and unique,
I melt, feeling the closeness to your skin.
I can't tell where I end, and you begin.
The touch of you, a journey of mystique!

So perfectly aligned and so in sync,
I feel you all around me, and all mine—
A sense of heaven, a glimpse of divine…
To me, wonderful man, you feel like silk!

Lusciously playful, timeless, subtle, free—
A love designed by you, defining me.

To hold and adore

I love you to tears,
Through sorrows and pain!
I love you with passion,
With you, I'm insane!

For you are my magic,
My heart and my dream,
You're my inspiration,
My voice from within.

When you are around me
I blush and I smile,
I feel you, I breathe you,
And pray that you're mine.

I love you completely,
Like never before!
I want you forever,
To hold and adore!

Forever

A life ago, I met you.
I fell in passion so!
I lost you, loved you, found you.
I will never let go!

Wherever you are, sweet love,
Defying space and time,
Over again, for always,
I'll find you! You'll be mine!

I'll love you in a circle!
I'll breathe you more than air!
My heart, my piece of heaven,
I'll follow you, I swear!

I'm yours! Always will be!
My world, my dream-come-true,
Soul of my soul, my fire,
Now and forever—you!

Just you

For some it comes easy, it grows and it stays,
While most only find it in their dreams and prayers;
Illusion, it may be, or a point of view,
But I touched and held it: for me, love is you!

And in long, cold winters, when your mind's away,
When your heart is lonely, when you're old and grey,
As you sit and wonder which crossroad you missed
And what's left of life is… past tense, memories,

Somewhere far in mindset, in time and in space,
I'll remember your eyes, your smile, your embrace,
How your touch would melt me, and how much I do
Still, loving no other, want one man—just you.

You would think...

When his voice is enough to brighten your day
And the closeness you share takes your breath away,
When your heart beats faster just because he's there,
You would think it mattered, you would think he'd care.

When it takes one touch to melt you to the core,
From the man who moves you, the man you adore,
And you want the whole world to know you're a pair,
How can it not matter? How can he not care?

When you kiss his eyes and tell him he's The One,
Yet you feel him distant and cold, like he's gone,
You know it won't change and you'll never get there.
To him, you don't matter. You must stop to care!

My story

A sunny day in autumn, leaves falling on the street,
A little girl was walking, so innocent and sweet,
So long ago, so far, before she met you,
A girl I used to know, but no longer do.

After a smile, a look, she right away knew
She wouldn't be the same—she now lived for two.
Before she realized it, you took over her heart.
She thought she found her purpose, a meaning, a new start.

The life she had before you, it vanished with your touch.
She couldn't understand it! She felt she changed so much!
For in your arms a lover and a woman were born.
She saw it, but you didn't; you left, and she was torn.

She wanted to forgive you, but she didn't know how.
Her innocence was shattered; her heart was broken now.
And I can't help but wonder, to love you like I do
If I'm no longer yours... who am I, without you?

A blessing and a curse

The house was cold and empty. No silhouette in sight.
She was alone and listening to silence, in the night.
At night… that's when she'd find him. He'd hold her, in her dreams,
The sweet boy she had once known—her only love, it seems.

Love at first sight, and always. Her heart, her dream, her "One!"
She wanted him forever; he wanted space and fun.
She saw her future in him but let him go. You see…
He said they'd be together if it was meant to be.

She never tried to find him but longed for him, and prayed
That he should crave to see her, that he came back and stayed.
And year after year, she never could forget;
She'd love, she'd hate, she'd miss him… but she'd never regret.

In dreams they were together: in love— no games, no lies.
But morning always found her with tears in her eyes.
Oh, how she missed his presence! Oh, how she missed his touch!
The one who didn't want her; the one she loved so much!

So many years of waiting…. How awful, what a shame!
For she had loved a lifetime and she had loved in vain,
Missing a man who only existed in her mind,
Who still governed her thoughts and had shaped up her life.

She wished she knew him better—in life; she wished to see
At least a glimpse of whom she made him up to be.
But in her final moments, in tears and in pain,
A single thing she wanted: the chance to live again.

On your birthday

A heart that beats with yours,
A sweet love that is true,
Happiness and fulfillment
Is what I wish for you!

And as the years fly by,
As much as you'll be changed,
Remember all those people
Whose lives you've rearranged;

For whom a smile of yours
Lights fires and shakes worlds,
Writes futures, pasts and presents
Onto their lives' white boards.

Know that you're loved by many,
Beyond limits and size.
You touch hearts, you have power.
Use it gently... be nice!

And as you reach your vision,
When success is in sight,
Throughout late nights of hard work
Try not to miss your life!

I wish you joy and laughter,
No choices to regret,
And hope this year brings you
Moments you won't forget.

The teacher

He held their hands as children, he raised them to stand tall,
Inspired them to reason, work hard and give their all.

From him they learned commitment, discipline and respect.
He showed them calm and patience and taught them to reflect.

A man whose heart's a treasure, whose words lit up their mind,
Whose wisdom knows no limits, who leaves no one behind;

His words won't be forgotten, nor will his kind, true eyes,
His teachings, that have brought greatness into their lives.

For he built their foundation and all throughout their path,
They'll know him as the mentor who deeply touched their heart.

And so we all stand here, us, that you've brought so far,
To say you make us better and have shaped who we are!

Deception

He caught her eye and charmed her
With what she thought to be
The sweetness of his character,
Passion and honesty.
As she took one step closer
The man she thought she'd seen
Had no physical presence:
Smoke and mirrors—a dream!

The one who'd tell her stories;
"The One", put on the spot,
He was her mind's reflection,
He wasn't who she thought!
A man who had no honor,
No feelings, and as such,
A shallow, empty person,
Who loved himself too much!

She wished she never met him!
She wished she could erase
How he'd dismiss her feelings
And made her mind a maze;
How he had dared to treat her
As if she were an object,
And all the anxious feelings
She wasted on the subject!

Handsome man

You, handsome man, whose eyes ignite with passion,
Whose touch and kisses tear my soul apart,
Invite me in your life! Let me get closer!
Let me see who you are and see your heart.

I want to be allowed to know you better;
I want your trust and demand your respect!
I want for you to treat me like a lady;
I want to be with you—I'll be direct.

Maybe if you allowed it, it'd be easy;
Maybe you'd find a feeling that's sublime.
A whole new world is possible, in "maybe".
Maybe you'd even learn to love, this time.

You ask to wait and see; you ask for patience.
You say your heart might open and seek mine.
I don't believe your promise, or your kisses,
And coming from your lips, I don't trust time.

I trust you'll say the words to get you places…
I trust you have no value for the truth!
I trust you're not for me, and someday, handsome,
I trust I'll find a new man, who is good.

My Someone

How can I close a chapter, end a tale long begun?
How can I call it "over" when I think you're The One?
Letting love conquer reason, you, in whose arms I run,
Give my sorrows a purpose, are my home, my Someone.

But with words that are hurtful, too deep is the harm done
And this side of you injures, cuts and burns like the sun.
How it stabs through my stomach when you laugh and I cry!
How I wish not to see it—hopes, illusions that die!

Look at me, foolish person, living life in my dreams,
Blind to *is*, always chasing what *could be*, what *it seems*!
Lost and gone are, forever, all those years I missed,
And I wonder, my Someone, if you even exist.

Too late

At some point, she stopped fighting. At last, she said: "Enough!"
And letting go of "True Love", promised she'd learn to laugh.
One day she would be happy. Above all, love herself!
The pain and tears—one day—she'll forget, on a shelf.

And time had passed…. Years later, in front of her: a ghost!
How unfair and ironic… the one she loved the most!
He looked at her as always; same smile that made her sink.
She didn't melt down this time. She didn't even blink!

She wondered, as she saw him, like through a broken glass,
Faded, just as their story, long gone, covered in dust,
If he, their love, her feelings, emotions buried deep,
If they were ever real or happened in her sleep.

This man, once so familiar, who would make her heart bleed,
Now, nothing but a statue whose eyes she couldn't read,
He didn't understand it. He, who believed in Fate,
He knew now that he loved her, but he came back too late.

The past

It lives to write the story
Of us,
But flies like leaves from trees,
Like dust,
To shape and round up memories—You'd think.
If only those old pictures
Could speak….

We find our strength and legacy
In it,
Although at times it makes us
Lose sleep.
It's good and bad, it's all things that
We've done;
It's how we've been and who we have
Become.

Perception of brief instances
And yet,
The root cause of our action, thought,
Regret.
To honor all those years
Gone fast,
Who would we be without it:
Our past?

Beauty in motion

Outside, snowflakes are playing in circles,
But to her it feels warm and it's peace.
So still, she can hear them speaking.
They fall to the tip of her fingers
And melt, but their memory lingers.

They talk of their journey through seasons,
The lives they touched and polished, how they've been
Material, spirit, weightless, solid, liquid. In stages,
To life's book, they attached their pages.

For every shape and form wraps an experience,
A joy of senses, a display of might;
Beauty in motion—snowflakes and our life.

Inside, life is playing in circle.
It's fluid, moving, wonderful… immortal.

Write again

The years passed; she waited.
She was tired and blue.
She loved and wanted someone
All wrong for her, she knew.
She lost her inspiration,
Her smile, the drive to live.
She felt alone and empty,
With nothing left to give.

The couples, when she'd see them,
They'd laugh, hold hands and play.
She forgot what that felt like,
But swore she'd know, one day!
And then, most unexpected,
She found a heart so mild,
Who saw her as a wonder,
A woman and a child.

His eyes had touched her deeply:
They were kind and had soul;
They mirrored deep emotions—
His eyes showed him as whole.
In his arms, she was little,
But strong—queen in her reign!
She smiled and she was grateful,
And she could write again.

Resolution

A year gone, and my new life at start;
A time to watch sad memories depart.
Life starts today, with nothing in the past.
This year is to focus, act and trust.

No happiness outside of me I'll seek!
No promises I'll make and never keep!
Serene, wonderful dreams only I'll host!
To inspiration and sublime I toast!

Enjoying every second, as it comes,
Gone is the girl that submits and succumbs!
No more walking my every step in fear!
I'll own and I'll design my life, this year!

Aware and open, joy I will create;
With sunshine, play and fun I will relate.
The only voice that matters—mine—I'll hear!
It honors and belongs to me, this year!

A parent and their child

So many things we blame them for, and fights we can't let go…
How we forgot that it is them who taught us all we know!
So much resentment that we've built, just so we can be right.
How little we acknowledge how much they were forced to fight!

They put their lives on hold for us and somehow we lost sight
That it took sacrifice and pain to raise another life!
We loved them, then, when we were young, no matter what the stakes.
We're adults now and changed the rules: heroes can't make mistakes!

Just think how many times we judged, imagine how they hurt,
To give their best, their all, themselves… gift beauty, receive dirt.
What if they only scream at us when they feel they have failed?
What if sometimes they're human too, and they get lost and scared?

Maybe we've been a bit unfair… maybe it's time to see
Not how and who they've been *to us*, but simply who *they* be!
Maybe we could try harder too, and we could be more mild,
For what could be more sacred than a parent and their child?

Letter (I missed that you were great!)

It's funny how we find someone who's sweet and kind and cute…
As soon as we can call them "mine", they're harsh and mean and rude!
Isn't that crazy, how it works? Same pattern, every time!
And then we go and tell our friends: "He changed when he was mine!"

Ever so often, one thought comes to our minds, briefly:
"What if it's me, not him? Oh gosh… I'm awesome, it can't be!"
But *it is* us, sometimes; we try to make them what we want
And we miss out on who they are, focused on what they're not.

It's sad to realize because these people we *don't* see,
They have a heart and dreams and hopes of all that they could be!
We don't support them, but complain, and blame them for the world!
And then we wonder why they've turned resentful, closed and cold.

I did it too… to you! I judged… I missed the harm I caused!
I failed to listen and observe I wasn't who I posed!
So now I'm writing just to say there were mistakes I made.
And in the process, I missed you! I missed that you were great!

When we're gone

You know how, when we're gone, they talk? We're popular, at last!
Too bad we can't attend! I bet we would have quite a blast!
Exciting stories of ourselves, from hors d'oeuvres to the cake.
Maybe they happened, maybe not… what difference does it make?

But those we touched and moved, they
grieve! They feel crippled and lost!
They want us back, just for a day! A day, at any cost!
Or some will say: "I knew her well: she smiled when she was sad,
Had a kind word for everyone, I never saw her mad."

Or "She was stubborn, she was proud, and at times even odd,
But she meant well…. I can't forget, she deeply touched my heart!
'Cause she had courage and had strength to just stay who she was,
When she felt pushed and trapped and scared, walked over or abused."

These people cared; they are the ones who brought us in their lives.
Because of them, we got to be best friends, mothers and wives!
And for the rest, don't you get sad! Nobody really knows…
They weren't there to share our paths and we're more than it shows.

You let them talk, because you know you always tried your best,
And you were giving and played fair, with honor, in life's test!
It doesn't matter what they say and how they make you look!
They're human too, and underneath, we're mellow, and we're good!

Little friend

Our little friends that teach us lessons…
If only they were heard!
If we were present every moment
To see the gifts they hold…

I wish I had a voice that caught me
When my thoughts wander wild,
To bring me back to you, to listen,
To step out of my mind,

Be there when you are scared and lonely,
Above to help you rise!
No need for words to tell your story,
It's written in your eyes!

If I look deeply, in an instant,
I see a heart of gold!
I see humanity and fear,
I see a child… and love.

Most patient and forgiving creature
Whose pain is left untold,
From you, I understood devotion
And honest, kind support!

I am so grateful to have had you,
To be your family!
Your lessons matter! You are treasured,
Most precious part of me!

We wait

We find ourselves trapped on a side road,
Resign and call it "Fate".
We turn to Time as our savior,
And wait.

Maybe it's Destiny… or Karma,
Mistakes our parents made.
Until the culprit makes its entrance,
We wait.

Meanwhile, as friend, we have self pity.
For company, complaint.
We criticize. We are the cynics.
We wait.

We don't like others when they're happy.
We simply can't relate.
We wish them hardships and some tears.
And wait.

Until they're served, we show them envy.
Sometimes, we hurt them straight.
Expecting freedom from frustration,
We wait.

At times, not often, conscience hits us
And there starts the debate.
We now feel guilty, but it passes.
We wait.

And tired, after years of waiting,
When we think it's too late,
We see no point in starting over.
We wait.

That's us… but others have a vision
And a life they create.
They're joyous and fulfilled and different!
They don't wait.

The people we meet

Some people we meet, we don't get, we don't feel;
Their image we quickly forget,
While some we bring back as a thought or a smile,
Nice people, to whom we relate.

We also meet those that we like and invite
To come and perform on our stage.
And although good actors, the play often pales
When words are just words on a page.

We meet special people: our mentors, our guides;
They come from our past and have stayed,
The people we treasure, who are in our lives,
Strong bonds and close friendships we've made.

And if we are lucky, and if we are blessed,
And if we can handle the ride,
We're given the one we will love beyond all,
The dart that gets stuck deep inside!

This one is the one where all judgment is lost,
The bet that we cannot afford,
The drug we now need just to keep us alive,
The reason our friends are appalled!

This is the bullet that slashes our hearts!
This is the scar that won't close!
With this one, we're torn, broken open and hurt!
It's torture, from head to the toes!

With this one, a year can feel like a day!
Without him, a day feels a year!
A million emotions a moment rush through,
From awe to despair and to fear!

With this one, we know we have loved and know pain;
With this one, we feel we have lived!
What wonders will happen when we take a chance
And *let in* the people we meet!

Little love

Little children, no fear—remember?
Vows we whispered in awe, in a game…
How we played and held hands,
How we fought, were best friends,
How we kissed, and it wasn't the same.

Thinking back, I still feel the emotions…
Little love… got us trapped in its spell!
Got us hit, got us bruised,
Didn't know what it was,
'Til it stopped at the sound of the bell.

I imagined my life would be over!
After you, there was nothing… but cold!
Something new was beginning,
Turned to beauty in being,
Led to me, more mature and bold.

But the young innocence disappeared.
Such is life: 'til you lose, you don't gain.
We grew up and we bloomed,
Our fire consumed,
How I wish we were little again!

Sweetest memory

It may be over, but you're not forgotten!
I'll be thinking of you, I'll be near.
I may not see you often, maybe ever,
But the closeness we shared, it was real.

I can't imagine life without you in it!
I never thought to you, I would say "no".
But if by having me, your dreams will perish,
To give your dreams a chance, I let you go.

I can't be good for you, if you're not peaceful.
You don't laugh anymore; it's been a while…
One day, try to forgive me if I hurt you;
I give you up, so I can see you smile.

I do love you, wholeheartedly, forever!
And when you love, nothing is asked or due.
A lifetime around you would make me happy;
I'd spend my every second knowing you!

So never wonder if you are remembered,
Because you touched my life, you're part of me!
And if our paths should cross, throughout our journey,
You'll still be loved… my sweetest memory!

For a dream

They seam so unattainable, so great,
For little me, and others who relate.
What use to dream for us? We're fraud, we're bait!
Winners have a uniquely special trait.

But what if little us can do great things?
What if we can move mountains with our dreams?
What if we tried to fly and grew the wings?
What if, in little us, lie queens and kings?

For certain, we would have to take a chance.
We'd give up comfort, yes, but we'd advance.
Like babies we would crawl, then walk, then dance.
Could it be? Do we even dare to glance?

Where would we start? We'd notice when we're moved.
Our dreams exist as passions, plain and crude.
They'd have to be our water, air and food.
Oh God, it'd be like living in the nude!

We could create something that's never been!
We'd give it all, we'd live life in extreme.
But if we failed, then what? What would that mean?
It'd mean we fought with courage, for a dream.

One of you

At times, it looks as though you're all alone.
Like you're invisible, non-critical, unknown;
Like challenges you face can't be surpassed,
And future, somehow, looks just like the past.

Life seems too hard; you feel tired and small.
Dreams you envisioned once, they now seem dull.
Your mental dialogue is stale and sad.
It isn't even worth it to be mad.

You think you're here for you… What if you're not?
What if you're endless, but think you're a dot?
What if it's miracles that your hands hold?
What if, reaching one soul, you touch the world?

Acknowledge who you are, what you've been through!
It took a lot of work to become you!
Don't change! You're wonderful! There's nothing wrong!
To some, you are like lyrics to a song.

In the whole world, one person lived your life.
One person learned your lessons, fought your fight.
That person can lift hearts, sharing their view.
In the whole world, there's only one of you!

I promise you!

I promise you, you have my heart!
I'll never run away!
I promise I will hold your hand
When we are old and grey!

I promise I belong to you!
I promise you respect!
I promise you that, looking back,
You'll say: "I don't regret!"

I promise that, to see you smile,
I'll do all that I can!
I'll be a cutie and a goof,
For you, beautiful man!

I promise I will honor you,
How you feel, who you are!
I promise you that, when you sigh,
I never will be far!

I promise to help you design
The life we'll walk towards!
With all I am, I promise you,
I love you, beyond words!

I promise I will be a stand
For you to always win!
To win in life, to win in love,
To feel at peace, within.

I promise you, my treasured soul,
A love that never dies!
You'll see yourself, your life, your dreams…
You'll see it, in my eyes.

And most of all, I promise you,
A love no-matter-what!
Because in you, I found, my love,
More than I'll ever want!

She loves

The sun has set in silence.
It's chilly. The wind blows.
She doesn't mind the raindrops.
She loves.

"He should be home" she's thinking
As she puts on her clothes.
In minutes, she'll surprise him—
She loves.

Her steps are girly, joyful,
She's itching in her toes!
She'll see him soon, the honey
She loves.

She speaks to every person,
Who stops her, that she knows.
She's cheerful, kind and smiley—
She loves.

She generates fulfillment.
Her eyes sparkle, she glows.
"What's up with you?" they ask her.
She loves.

"I'm grateful that I met him!
He is the path I chose.
He's gentle!" she tells people.
She loves.

"Love should be light and easy.
When it's right, it all flows.
It's peaceful!" she continues.
She loves.

She says: "Goodbye!" and giggles,
"I love… I guess it shows."
She waves. Her man is waiting.
She loves.

In the garden she passes,
She stops to smell a rose.
"Smells sweet like him" she whispers.
She loves.

"I'd love him for a lifetime,
No matter what arose!
He's meant for me! He's lovely!"
She loves.

She stops just for a second
To catch her breath. She knocks.
He smiles. Her voice is shaky.
She loves.

She says: "I missed you, baby!"
He waits as the doors close.
"You're mine!" he says and hugs her.
She loves.

Hear the rain

I've given up my dream of us, together,
And for the first time, there's no one to blame,
And I can think of you and read our letters,
And even talk of us and say your name.

Who would have thought… after so many years?
I sooner would have died, than let you go!
The more I tried, the more you didn't love me.
I'm finished fighting and accept what's so.

It's quiet now. There's space, all of a sudden.
Feels like the spice is gone and life is plain.
Nothing to cry about and it's confusing:
What is it people do when there's no pain?

All of this stillness… I don't understand it!
And all these people that I haven't seen…
Looks like they know my life and have suggestions.
Somehow, they seem to know where I have been.

They try to help, but all I hear is judgment.
Why can't they go away, and let me sink?
I wonder if they know that I am grieving.
I wish they gave me time, so I can think.

A life to live… alone… a heart in pieces…
There must be others who've hurt and pulled through!
I don't know how, but I choose to consider
That I will find a way to move on too.

Maybe the spice is gone—forever even,
But now there's peace, and in this space… who knows?
Maybe life must be so, to teach us lessons.
Maybe this is the way a person grows.

I miss the dream of love—the dream of Fairies.
I miss your touch and the exquisite pain!
But what a gift and such delightful freedom
To just be *here*, and hear the rain!

I've given up my dream of us, together,
And for the first time, there's no one to blame.
And I can think of you and read old letters,
And be amazed… at how strong I became!

Stop

Fighting with "What if...?" made me think I'm crazy
And all because I believed in a man!
Some said I've chosen comfort and I'm lazy;
"No self-esteem!" they said, and so I ran.

Not from the man—I loved him! From the voices;
I ran from friends, from people, from the world.
With what right do they criticize my choices?
Who do they think they are, to say I'm wrong?

They called me desperate, and naive—they called me!
They said I chase dreams to escape the truth.
I heard "belittled", "small", in how they saw me,
And ran where there was nothing to be proved.

One option left: alone... me and my bruises.
It's suffocating when you're this alone!
I couldn't count on you and found excuses.
The weight of life, the fear, had me thrown.

And one sweet afternoon, my sweet boy told me:
"I hope I get to meet somebody new!"
That's how the veil was lifted, and it hit me
How much I wasted in waiting for you.

See… wanting someone so much you can feel it
Has one blind to the greatness of the cost.
One fights so hard! They are a cause, they be it!
Before they know it, they're consumed and lost.

And I fought hard because I felt diminished,
And hit the bottom, diving from the top.
But I have power now to call it *finished*,
To say I did my best, and now I stop.

The code of love

He'd smile and say: "I love you!" Then he'd kiss me.
He'd hold me tight and tell me: "I'm your man!"
But say "relationship" and he'll go missing.
He'll run as fast and as far as he can!

Often, he'd say: "I miss you, honey-baby!
I think of you before I go to sleep."
But then he'd never call. He'd be too busy.
And how can one get mad? Look! He's so sweet:

"I want to be so close! I want you, baby!
I'm sad without you! Life is dry and black.
I'm tired to go out, but you come over!
Let's watch TV and you can scratch my back!"

"He's really into me!" one would be thinking;
"He calls me "honey", he thinks that I'm sweet!
He likes to have me close, see? I'm his baby!"
Ask him to take me out—he gets cold feet.

Forget meeting the parents—he's not ready.
The word "exclusive" also makes him run.
Talk about future, and you lost his interest.
Show him a ring, it's like he sees a gun!

God help me if I say the word "commitment"!
Such terrible mistake! Such a dead road!
Why must it be like this, so complicated?
Why not provide translation for his code?

If words say one thing and actions another,
Mastering what he means becomes an art!
What do you trust? How do you know what's real?
How does a girl manage to win his heart?

Because I choose

So, I'm emotional and you are not.
You're Mr. Rational, I'm burning hot.
So, we are different… what is there to do?
No chance for us? Not meant to be? Says who?

When I share what I feel or what I need,
You hear I demand and try to lead.
You feel the menace lurking in unseen;
I feel that you're my heart, my greatest dream!

So, we won't change, but I don't want us to!
I like the way we are! I'm choosing you!
And we can make a deal, you and me both:
To not assume but ask—this is our oath!

I'll make the rule that only I hurt me,
That I can suffer, but don't need to be.
The other rule is that we are both good.
If it looks different, we misunderstood.

There will be bumps along the way, that's life.
We make the context—that's why we'll survive.
I vow to love you and not let us lose,
Because I have a dream, because I choose.

To love

I've loved you in my dreams, for long, I've loved you from afar…
Those eyes that smile, your touch of silk—I love the man you are!
I crave for you like you're a drug! To love you is a sin!
I'd spend forever in your arms, with your scent on my skin!

To have you… what wouldn't I give! All I am, all I know!
I'd put you first, nourish your soul; I'd live to see you glow!
I'd hold you tight and comfort you when you feel in defeat;
You give me joy! You are the man who makes my life complete!

I'd cherish you and our love! I'd give up being right!
I'd leave the past where it belongs to have you in my life!
And if my heart I open now is to show you my world,
For you to see if you belong and let your mind unfold.

I want you free, with wings to fly! I want for you to choose,
To know you live the life you want, your dreams to never lose!
Say "yes" and I belong to you; say "no" and I'll forgive.
Because to love, it means to hurt, and above all… to give.

The woman I've become

I met you as a girl—now I'm a woman.
Because of you, of the man that you are!
You taught me how to love and how to listen.
It is because of you I got this far!

With generosity, you let me know you
And altered my experience of life.
You showed me things I missed, that I was blind to.
Because of you, what stopped me, came in sight.

I learned from you the lesson of acceptance,
I learned how to forgive, how to be kind.
You taught me how it feels when one shares closeness.
I found renewed respect for a man's mind.

Never before have I felt this much passion!
I understood how deeply a man loves;
How intimate, how honest and how open
My love will be, when I stop fighting wars.

I saw that when one loves, they feel inspired;
They're hopeful and unguarded, like a child.
I would have missed it all, had you not shown me
Your eyes could be this trusting and this mild.

For what you've done for me, for what you gave me,
For teaching me to see a different way,
I thank you from my heart, because of your coaching
I never will be able to repay!

I met you as a girl—now I'm a woman!
All due to you… to the man that you are.
You've helped me grow! Because of you, I'm better
And see with pride the woman I've become!

In giving up

In giving up "It is the way I know!"
I'd get to be surprised and awed and moved;
I'd live from what's created, not improved;
I'd have an open space to be, to grow.

In giving up the meaning of the words,
I'd get to hear only what was said.
The words would flow, they'd dance inside my head;
They'd be so light, they'd fly away like birds.

In giving up that someone is at fault,
That I re-live the past, that something's wrong,
I'd get to access an amazing world:
Perfection that existed by default.

In giving up "This is how it should be!"
I'd see the beauty that lies in what is,
The honesty that stands behind a kiss,
I'd love and share and dream… I would be free!

In giving up the doubt, the looking back,
I'd be courageous, take risks and believe;
What a surprising thought: optional grief—
Possible in the space of giving up.

Be right

This picture looks familiar;
I've seen it all before:
Life happens, she gets frightened,
Walks out and slams the door.

In this one situation
And many that have been,
She'll try to not look hopeless;
She'll pass… go home and dream.

Whenever she's unsure,
Uncomfortable, at test,
She'd rather give up outright,
Than not be at her best.

This way she's not confronted,
She's safe, has the last word,
She can't be touched, she's solid
And avoids being told.

In this scene, she has power,
She dominates, she's right;
When she's alone, there's no one
To make her wrong, to fight.

And she sees what she misses,
She knows she pays a cost;
She's clear: in her choices,
There's something that she lost.

She lost the hope, she's lonely,
Her dreams are not alive;
Her friends, her social being,
She put it all aside.

But if she finds good reasons,
For as long as she can,
She'll pass on love, achievements,
Just to follow her plan.

And people will live lifetimes
With arguments and pride,
And say "no" to their loved ones
Just so they can be right.

A good heart

"Not with me!" as you put it—
We were not in the stars.
And I heard that as story,
I was blind to the scars.

But I get, now, the feelings
Of despair and defeat,
And the numbness and nausea,
How they cut through my feet.

How it feels to be empty,
Drained of hope, lacking strength,
Staring aimless, in darkness,
Linking loving to death.

To be crushed so profoundly,
So exhausted, so weak,
Paralyzed, suffocating,
And unable to speak!

I expect in my lifetime
I will not understand
How a love, to me breathless,
Was to you, blowing sand.

All that's left, at these crossroads,
Is for me to accept
You'll remain in my make-up
As defining event.

You'll exist as my teacher
Due to whom I learned pain,
And a blood stamp, forever,
To my heart and my brain.

I'll accept that I suffered,
But I'll never deny:
You're a beautiful person;
A good heart… so am I.

Who knows?

Who's there to say I could have made you whole?
That I'd have gotten in, to melt your soul?
Who can conclude I would have loved you most?
Maybe apart is best for both… who knows?

Who knows, maybe the timing wasn't right;
Maybe we tried too hard, we held too tight;
Maybe it's time to let go and repose;
Maybe this is our Destiny… who knows?

Maybe we gave too little, or too late;
Maybe we were just good, but weren't great.
We go in circles, think, wonder, suppose…
The end of story's open… no one knows.

Maybe apart we will encounter peace;
Maybe what we called "love" was a caprice.
In time, the pain will heal, the wounds will close.
Maybe then we'll find happiness… who knows?

Love by design, forgiveness by choice

When I love you by choice and not based on the norm,
When I'm slow to react, but rethink and transform,
If I see our love as a gift, as Divine,
What is real for me, is a love by design.

If I know I'm not stuck, but I'm strong and I choose,
And reserve for myself the free will to refuse,
I am clear from angst, free to live in today,
With no questions or doubts that "The One" slipped away.

When you cause me to cry and I choose to forgive,
Giving up blaming you, making room to believe,
I allow you to grow, in your life, in my eyes,
To be more than your past, a potential surprise.

In the end, sweetest heart, love will hurt just because
We are human, not Gods, we have goodness and flaws.
In our life, and in love, *what* will be, we can't choose,
But we choose *who* to be, *how* to act, and our views.

Melt

"I miss you, love you, want you always…" and promised you I'd stop.
Is it the feeling, so consuming, or words over-the-top?
Big, overwhelming words that trap us, words that conclude what is,
When substance fades and interactions feel like you're being quizzed.

I promised you my heart forever—even those, words that fly.
What is "forever"? Seven letters and an intrinsic lie.
I know no words to show you, sweetheart, to what my love amounts,
No words express a world of feelings—not in a way that counts.

So don't expect my love in language—don't know it when it's said!
Words may be meaningless, misleading, and many times, misread.
I trust you'll know it, at the right time, not as a point of view,
But as a feeling in your body, simply because you do.

Stop putting reason in emotions, and in reason, control!
It's meant to flow and to fulfill you, not to fulfill a goal.
It's easy, really… love just happens. It's not induced, it's felt.
My body knows it loves you, honey, because you make me melt.

I pray

I'd talk to you, but you can't hear me; I'd write, but you can't see.
The love I feel with all my being exists only for me.
And when my eyes get filled with tears, late at night, in my bed,
When I can't tell you that I love you, I talk to God instead.

I tell Him what you wouldn't hear, what you don't want to know,
Because He'll listen without judgement and He won't say: "Let go!"
And He won't tell me, like you'd tell me, as a matter of fact,
That love is silly, and in this world, love is just not enough.

I ask Him why He would allow a world where love won't win;
How is it wrong to feel my feelings, at the touch of your skin?
And now when we have reached an impasse, with nothing left to say,
I kneel in humbleness and ask Him to help me breathe… I pray.

I pray for you to find that something that moves you beyond words,
That makes you want to become better, that makes your life a cause,
That gives you strength, so you discover the
things you thought you knew,
I pray you find the joy and blessing that I have found in you.

And when I pray for you, my honey, I don't ask that you're mine;
I ask for you to find your purpose, inspiration and smile.
I pray to hear that you're happy and that your dreams came true,
Even if life has moved you forward, and you're with someone new.

Apart

They didn't just move on. They thrive.

They've built fulfilling homes, new lives,
From rules that, at the time, seemed wise,
And so, they live each day.
And they're ok.

Apart, but still in love—deeply attached.

Impassioned through a time that wouldn't fly,
Experiencing that hearts don't lie,
And passion doesn't die,
Despite one's try.

Apart, and silently, always together,

In prayers, in dreams, in light—
Just not in life.
Each carrying the other in their heart,
Connected, but apart.

Apart, they learned people can't be replaced,

The past can't be erased,
And love, you can't outsmart.
Yet, they're ok.
Apart.

Time

How years pass and how we change, while always staying us;
How we transform—or try, at least—what we think, do, discuss;
How we look back and single out those times when we fell short—
What we would give to wipe it clean, go back, those times to thwart!

How blessed are we, to meet again! Back to the scene of crime,
I'm terrified we'll fail once more in relating to time.
It wasn't them, it wasn't me, or your protective gear,
Not differences, not lack of love, just a whole lot of fear!

And I've looked back at the pain caused, at the scars that were earned;
I see it now in a new light, and this is what I've learned:
The greatest loss, that tears one's soul, the kind that makes us kneel—
There's nothing breath won't get us through!
There's nothing time won't heal.

The cruelty, the disrespect, the behaviour of fools—
In dealing with the aftermath, I adopted new rules:
To breathe and pause and not react, the anger to release,
Above all goals, above all wants, to value my own peace;

That, to gain peace, it is my mind that must obey my heart;
That I will need to face my ghosts and piece them all apart;
That I must willingly submit and invite you to lead
And learn to be and deal with thoughts that angst and anger feed.

In doing this, in being calm and able to collect,
That's where I'll find my deeper self, my inner voice, my strength.
Accepting, with an open heart, committed to receive,
On any path you'll lead me through, I know I will succeed.

And as for you, I trust you, now! I know you from within.
I'll look, in you, for good and right, support you, help you win
With me, *or* her, with what *you* need! I won't oppose, for I'm
Aware all happens as it should—nothing before its time.

Authentic love

I remember once you told me—and receiving it, was tough—
That love, while it may have meaning, it is simply not enough.
So, I wonder, with more wisdom and desire to succeed:
Can I make you happy, baby? Can I give you what you need?

Can I help you become better? Do you find yourself through us?
Could I earn your full commitment and your everlasting trust?
Would you lead me, would you train me, would you teach me what to do
To fulfill you, to complete you, and bring out the best in you?

If it's me, I'd spend forever finding ways to make you smile;
If you share more with another, you and I are not worthwhile.
Because when you end your journey, I would like you to attest
Beyond doubt, concerns or questions, that life offered you the best.

I love you so much, it scares me, and your happiness comes first
Even if it means to lose you; not fulfilling you is worse.
But I've loved you for a lifetime and as long as I'm alive,
I will pray to be your woman and the love in which you thrive.

I'll be here for you always, and whatever choice you make,
I'll support you; I won't tell you that you're making a mistake.
And I may not have all answers, but this one thing I know of:
There can never be, my honey, a more true, authentic love.

Can't let go

You've found your way back to my life;
So much has changed, except my heart—
As if we've never been apart,
As if it didn't feel your knife
When you assessed I'm not your wife;

It keeps you wrapped inside its core,
Entangled with its every beat;
In loving you, it feels complete.
My heart needs you and nothing more;
Your love will help it heal and soar.

I'm learning how to vocalize,
For so long, having lost my voice—
Per the instructions of your choice—
I've heard the silent compromise
When one survives, but their soul dies.

You are what brightens up my day!
Forever in my soul engraved—
There's no escape, I am enslaved.
But *you* must choose... I can just pray.
Don't let me go! Please, stay! Please… stay!

How you are now, I wouldn't know;
There's truly nothing I expect;
Your every choice I will respect;
To me, you're pure light, you glow.
I feel your soul. I can't let go!

Before You take him back

My dear Lord, my precious God, it's me, Your tested child
Who used to kneel in dark, cold nights, who'd ask You to be mild
To an ill man, but whom I loved, to find him where he'd roam,
To keep him safe and guide his steps and bring my daddy home.

It's me, who asked: "Please, stay a while!" when You were all I had,
When I felt lonely, low on hope, when I was scared and sad.
You brought him home; you stayed with me;
my faith You helped preserve;
You gave me strength and pushed me through when I didn't deserve.

And now I'm back, my dear God, to ask for Your decree,
To beg for mercy and for grace; I'm back with a new plea
To ask You, God, because You're *Love* and I know You are kind:
How should I rightly live my life when, to your plan, I'm blind?

You, dear God, gave me this man; You put him in my view.
I know You want him in my life! He brings me close to You.
When he is near, I feel joy; without him, I am half.
I feel that when he speaks to me, he speaks on Your behalf.

You know how much I've yearned for him! You've counted every tear.
You've heard my thoughts and You, alone, silenced their voice of fear.
When, through his curtains, I made out his new love's silhouette,
You, God, and only You were there and You know how I wept.

You are my witness and You've seen how my heart mourned and bled;
How I begged You to make it stop, choking in tears shed.
I prayed: "Don't let me hate him, God, and her, don't let me hate!
Help me move on! Don't shut my heart! Please, let me live, not wait!"

And so You did, merciful God, and more than I had hoped,
You've brought him back! And in pure love
my mind and soul are soaked.
So now I'm writing to implore: please, God, let our love win!
And more than anything, please, God, don't declare it a sin!

Look at him now, my treasured man: beautiful, inside-out;
More mellow, open hearted, soft... You've picked the perfect route.
But if his soul is mine, please God, give this love one last glance!
I'm not requesting "'til the end", I'm begging for one chance.

Through tears and time, I promise, God, I love him ever more!
With every fiber of my heart, I beg and I implore:
You took him then... please, not again! But, if he starts to pack,
Please let me hold him one more time... before You take him back!

All of me loves all of you

I love you, and I will love you, for as long as I exist!
All of life fell in the background from the moment we first kissed.
When you're gentle, kind and loving *or* creating thunderstorms,
Playful, sweet, crude, rough or reasoned— I love you in all your forms!

All I wish for you is: magic! If you're happy, I'm at peace.
All I pray for is to know you, know the half of heart I miss.
Loving you calms and fulfills me, makes me happy, burns my soul,
Melts my core and warms my being. Loving you, I become whole.

Yes, your choices caused me heartache, but I trust that if I knew,
If I saw your life, upbringing, learned the things that you hold true,
I would understand your vision, reasoning, and hope I would
Recognize your tough decisions maximized the greater good.

I believe in you, my baby! In my eyes you're a great man!
For my loss of faith, forgive me! There was beauty in His plan.
Although filled with tears and torment, it immensely helped me grow;
Wouldn't trade our past—our story—not for anything I know!

What a blessing to experience that my mind embraced the truth
Which my heart has known forever! God is merciful and good!
I'm empowered to acknowledge, proudly so, if I may add:
I belong to you, I'm yours, I'm enough! And I thank God

For the peace that filled my being when my inner struggles stopped;
For consoling and completing with your heart, my longing heart;
For, in loving you so deeply, I want, I need, nothing more.
You're my home, my heart's vibration and the man that I adore.

No one else can dig so deeply! No one challenges me so!
Please, my love... please God, I beg you, please, don't let him let me go!
No one else can make me better and I love him, God, I do!
Sweetheart of my soul, my honey, all of me loves *all* of you!

Trust

To kiss your lips, to feel your touch,
Get lost into your loving eyes,
That's what l want and need so much,
My love that never dies!

To see that smile that melts my heart,
Discover all that we could be,
That's what I need, that's what I want!
That smile's the end of me!

To hold your hand, to let you lead,
Make you feel loved in every way,
That's what I want, that's what I need,
To give, not take away.

To know you're well, be one, be close,
Try to contribute, help you win,
To give support, not to oppose,
I need to be let in!

Believe in me, I'm on your side!
When you feel sad, I feel your grief.
I'm here for you! Put down the wall!
Let me provide relief!

You're all I want, you're *all* I need!
This love will amplify and last.
For you, I pray, with you, I plead:
Give me your heart, your trust!

One

Not always does one have a chance to fully be oneself,
Attempting mostly to get by, by preference or compelled.
I'm grateful to know who I am, and at my very core,
There is a love which gives me life, a man who makes me whole;

There is a soul that lives in you—the other half of mine,
A man whose touches melt my heart; wrapped in your love, I shine.
I know and feel you from within; obeying you, I'm free.
By simply being who you are, you bring out more of me.

The One who taught me to express, be present and not plan,
The *only* One who knows my flaws and loves me as I am;
The One for whom my body burns and whose cuddles I crave,
The One to whom my heart belongs and will love to its grave;

Fulfilling and consuming love, my All, my spirit's call,
The constant presence, gentle vibe, the essence of my soul;
The One who brightens up my day, for whom I cry at night,
You put emotion in my heart and meaning in my life.

For what we've built, for all you give, for staying, when I ran,
For how you mold me with such grace, I treasure you, sweet man!
For how you love me, who you are, for all the good you've done,
I'm yours, baby, you're my pair—The One with whom I'm One.

One flesh, One soul, no boundaries; the only truth I know;
Complete devotion to my man whose closeness makes me glow;
Full trust, a bond so strong, so true, that nothing can displace,
I'm all for you, in a deep love, surpassing time and space.

Your nurturer, your property, like Play-Doh in your hands,
Your woman who, when all else fails, will hold a love that stands;
In every way, in all your forms, you're everything I want,
To give you pleasure, hold your hand, share life and heal your heart.

You have my loyalty, support, commitment and respect;
My word to love the ones you love, protect those you protect;
To honor you, help you succeed, cherish this love like none!
I'll never question, never quit! It's you and I—we're One.

Unmistakably whole

You don't say very much but I treasure each phrase
And I thank you for all that you share!
You inspire and lift me in so many ways!
Wrapped in you, I become more aware.

In your energy realm I attain a new me,
One that's happy, intensely alive.
It's my soul you awake, it's my heart you set free!
You enrich my perception of life!

I feel numb, absent you! When you're back, I'm in awe;
My heart smiles, thoughts of wisdom abound!
Every time, there's no doubt, it's an unwritten law:
I am better when you are around!

Fully me, breathing peace, intertwined with myself,
You bring out all I am, all I need!
Free of worry and thought and devoid of intent,
Loving you, I become so complete!

It's a miracle, magic, a blessing, such love,
Causing *one* and *the other* to melt
In a union, where judgements and egos must fold,
In the intimate sharing of self;

A surprise we don't vanish, but rather expand,
More secure in losing control—
In this space, close to you, with my hand in your hand,
I'm at home, unmistakably whole.

Pain over denial

This letter is to ask You, God,
To guide me when my mind gets flawed,
When I get trapped in fears and ghosts
And question what I need the most.

This letter is to ask for help
When I get scared and lose myself,
To calm me down and grant relief
When my heart drowns in disbelief.

I made mistakes! And so did he.
Neither was all that we could be.
And now, more wrinkled, feeling more,
Help us do better than before!

Help me not dread, but dwell in time;
Even apart, *know* that he's mine.
Help me be patient and keep faith,
Believe in him, breathe and just wait.

Allow me to embody grace!
Teach me to love him, match his pace,
Slow down, be present more, talk less,
Listen from space, from nothingness.

Whatever form our future takes,
Don't let me make the same mistakes!
Don't let me hurt him when I bruise!
Help me be better than I was!

Please God, connect me to his heart!
Help me not judge, push or react!
If he should struggle in his quest,
In him, let me bring out the best!

Let me recall he's my heart's pick;
That when I fight him, I feel sick;
That his soft touches heal and soothe;
That when he speaks, he speaks Your truth.

God, I know nothing of Your plan,
But I know him! I love this man!
He is who melts me with one kiss;
Let him be mine, God! I am his.

We had great lows, but greater highs.
I find my whole self in his eyes!
So, when it hurts, don't let me run!
Let me remember he's The One!

And as I question, as I hide,
Remind my heart: I'm on his side!
In all his forms! In every shape,
This is the love I won't escape!

This is the love where I'm alive.
When all else fails, it *will* survive!
Give me the strength to face its trial!
I'll take its pain over denial.

You are heard

When I say: "I miss you, honey!"
And you answer: "Tell me more!"
When I tell you that I love you
And you say: "I love you more!"

When you whisper: "I'm all yours!"
That for me you crave and long,
Baby, how I miss your kisses
And the arms where I belong!

When you say that love's an onion
And its layers make one cry,
I remember how you wrapped me
In a love I can't deny.

When you talk of our love making
As expression, I feel… well,
Like I melt, like my heart races;
Simply put, under your spell.

When you say our love is special,
That I give you butterflies,
I recall moments of closeness
And get tears in my eyes.

When you answer: "Tell me 'bout it!"
To my asking for your hug,
My heart yearns, my body shivers,
And I need you like a drug.

Your "no problems, just solutions"
Playful manner to advise
Warms my heart and makes me wonder
How have you become so wise?

When, to my recommendation
You respond: "No questions asked."
When you say: "First try, *then* worry!"
My heart smiles, like in the past.

Once, after a lengthy absence
With hands shaking, you spoke of
Your mistakes, regret and "what if…"
And a total, complete love.

But my favourite is the image
Of the "very hungry kid
In the candy store"—poor baby!
We imagine what he did!

I remember it all, honey!
I heard every single word!
What you say has weight and impact:
You are treasured! You are heard!

Because

"Because he lies", "because he cheats", "because he said...", or "did..."
Because he went against your wish, didn't discuss, but hid,
"Because of" this, "because of" that, "because of different views"
Whatever your "because" may be, "because" is an excuse.

Rather than using your "because" to justify your move,
Instead of focusing your thoughts on what his actions prove,
Do you think, maybe, from his side, he did the best he could?
And had he shared his truth with you, would you have understood?

Do you think you created space for him to self-express?
How much would you say is your share of the resulting mess?
Do you know a relationship is always made of two
And has it ever crossed your mind it's not all about you?

We all want love, but love implies to nurture, to let live;
Love is a promise to be friends, accept, and mostly give.
If it feels off, it's not "because" that should be your main aim—
See if, or where, you may improve. Don't be so quick to blame!

And if the two of you conclude it is beyond repair,
Don't make him be the enemy, but one for whom you care.
Preserve your power and your grace, choose what you want to cause:
A fresh start and a better life by *your choice*, not "because".

Happening now

Fast forward the years and stand at life's end—
Would you like how you lived? What would you amend?
Would you carry regrets or weight on your chest?
Would the partner you chose have mirrored *you* best?

Would you walk the same path, lay down the same bid?
Would the life that you built have looked like *you* did?
Would the choices you made be worth the breaths spent?
Would you have been fulfilled, or only content?

Would you reckon you owned it, felt self-expressed,
Confronted your shortfalls, attempted your best?
Would you stand by your deeds, by who you became?
Would you mentor your child to do it the same?

Step by step, word by word, our vision gets blurred...
Carve *your* mark, stand *your* ground and make *your* voice heard!
It's *your* journey, *your* artwork, to build, not to bow!
Time goes by, life is short and it's happening *now*.

Goodbyes

We're gathered here to say: thank you! To say you touched our hearts,
To wish you luck, as life is changing and a new chapter starts.
We're confident you know we love you, from Back Office to Tax.
As such, we don't intend to praise you, but just stick to the facts.

You have inspired us for years with your words and your brain
And taught us some VPs in Finance are basically… not sane.
Your courage to stand on the table and speak with a straight face
Is what has earned you in our memories and hearts, an honoured place.

We thank you for the pizza lunches you kindly entertained!
In years of diet, rest assured, we'll lose the weight we've gained.
We also thank you for the cookies and the coffees on Fridays
And promise not to hold against you that there were none on Mondays.

You taught us that, when lacking water, one mustn't be upset,
As, equally effective, Red Bull, produces heat and sweat.
And on this note I'll address briefly your journey to stay slim:
I must admit, it's been delightful to see you at the gym!

For forcing us, once every quarter, to privately converse
We wish to say we hold no grudges—monthly would have been worse.
For all those times when in deep secret we thought you to be odd,
We beg forgiveness from Thee, Sire, our genius and great sport!

We're gathered here to acknowledge our Commander Supreme:
You've proudly nurtured us and made us a World Class Finance Team!
Our dear Sir, it's been a pleasure! We say without remorse:
You'll be remembered for your kindness—and for your looks, of course.

To summarize your little wonders I haven't mentioned still:
The person coming to replace you will have large shoes to fill!
We're proud of you and love you dearly, Mr.
Kind Smile, Big Heart, Blue Eyes!
So, keep in touch! Don't be a stranger, 'cause we don't like goodbyes.

Happy Birthday to you!

There comes a time for every person,
A turning point in life,
When one must peacefully acknowledge
That youth is out of sight.

Eventually, it pardons no one,
For all of us it's due.
But for today, we're celebrating
The birthday girl—that's you!

We wish you wisdom, grace, and surely
(Not meaning to insult)
The calmness, humbleness, expected
Of a mature adult.

Leaving aside the jokes and teasing,
It's such an honor to
Be in the presence of your spirit
And share this day with you.

Such an inspiring, strong woman,
Whose smile lights up a room,
Don't be concerned, as someone like you,
With age can only bloom.

Don't ever change! Know that we love you!
With no further ado,
We want to say, beautiful lady,
Happy Birthday to you!

Thank you!

I couldn't leave and not acknowledge how much you've helped me grow!
I wouldn't go before I tell you "Thank you!" for the below:
Thank you for giving me the chance to make you change your mind
And being willing to consider I'm leadership inclined!

Thank you for treating me with kindness and showing me respect—
That precious attitude in life many tend to neglect.
Thank you for always making sure I feel like I belong,
And most of all, thank you for caring enough to ask: "What's wrong?"

For being willing to consider another's point of view;
For your support and listening, I truly do thank you!
Thank you for being a fair leader; for your integrity!
I think you're awesome and you rock—I mean… respectfully!

Don't get me wrong, working for you was not a piece of cake!
My head distinctively remembers a mild, but chronic ache.
But when I think of all you've taught me and what I take away,
I'd choose you over any leader on any given day!

I could go on, on many pages, but I'll conclude as such:
Thank you because I felt acknowledged—to me, that meant so much!
Thank you for being there to guide me in the years that flew!
I wouldn't be who I've become if I hadn't met you!

Our greatest gift

To each of my daughters

Our precious baby-princess, our little cutie-pie,
Heart of our heart, our angel, your mom and dad will try
In these brief lines to guide you, and somehow to address
The blessing you are to us, that words cannot express.

Please read through these few verses, forgive the clumsy rhymes,
Receive your parents' wisdom, remember it at times
When life may bring you challenge, when you may feel despair,
To hear your parents' voices when we may not be there.

We're writing to inspire, to take you deep within,
Connect you with your power, remind you where you've been,
Strengthen your faith and calmness, so when things go adrift,
You stand, strong as a mountain! You are our greatest gift!

Be always with our child!

To each of my daughters

You gave us such a blessing! We're happy and fulfilled!
With joy but also anguish our minds and hearts are filled.
So tiny and so fragile, we ask to give her strength
And pray to whom may listen: please shower her with health!

Please keep her in good spirits, in peace and love, in light!
Surround her with good people and make her future bright!
Put only happy tears in those luminous eyes!
Protect her, give her courage, make her agile and wise!

We ask that she be humble, successful in her life,
That she become a mother and a most treasured wife;
That You should guide her journey and make her upsets mild;
We pray to whom may listen: be always with our child!

What you're worth

To each of my daughters

And so, we had a baby: the precious, perfect you!
All that we used to value we instantly outgrew.
Each day we are so grateful we were given this gift
And pray to God to keep you, forever, just as sweet.

We want you to remember, always, never forget,
Regardless of surroundings, how changed or old you get,
How blessed we feel to know you; how great you're in our eyes!
We love you past our beings, through time, beyond demise!

But know that in your journey not everyone will see
Your spirit and your beauty and when it's hard, they'll flee.
Don't try to fix or change them! Don't bother to know why!
Remember that good people do not make others cry.

Let no one give you sorrow! Let no one treat you raw!
Your essence is too pure, with not a fault or flaw.
Give nobody permission to treat you like a toy!
Have faith and ask for blessings, because you bring life joy.

Make sure they respect you—the people that you meet;
That they kind and loving, that they don't lie or cheat;
That they are patient, humble, moral, hard working, deep;
That for you, they'd move mountains; that you're their everything.

92

Demand and be courageous, don't compromise or trade!
You're good and you're deserving—the best we've ever made!
Don't wait, because our hours are limited on Earth.
Choose Now, with strength and firmness! Remember what you're worth!

Beauty

To each of my daughters

You see them all painted, dressed up and plain fake.
They failed to discover for what, for whose sake.
They spend all their savings to buy creams and colors
And then to apply it, they further spend hours.

They struggle with eating to look like an actress—
They swear: "To get beauty, it takes pain and practice!"
And let us not mention the clothes, shoes and purses—
They think they're unique and they make their own choices.

Attempt to explain it as much as you would,
The concept of "beauty" is misunderstood.
To think one buys beauty is over simplistic;
It's not sold in stores, and it's not in a lipstick.

Producers have tricked them: it's not in their closets;
They made it effect so that they could sell causes.
It's not on the scale and it's not in a close-up,
It's there in your smile and it's there when you wake up;

It's there when you're peaceful, content and aware,
In gestures and actions of goodness you share;
It's there when you're happy, it shines through your gaze,
It fills us with joy and it warms up our days;

94

It's there when you know that your body is great
In whichever outfit and whatever shape;
When you know you're lovely without any help,
When you love, accept and honor yourself.

Beyond

To each of my daughters

Raw awareness to some,
Essence of what we are,
Nucleus of a star,
The place from where we come;

Totality that *is*,
The Universe, the Now,
Nothingness, love, a vow,
Un-manifested bliss;

To others, brilliant fraud;
A brainwashing technique
For the simple and weak;
Yet others call it God—

Creator of the world,
Goodness personified
We'll meet in afterlife
Our Father and our Lord.

Look deep inside to *see*
And find your inner truth.
Beliefs of other youth,
Allow them all to be.

Establish your own terms,
Accept, honor and give,
Be humble and forgive,
Love life in all its forms.

Be fair, be kind, have trust
To create, not respond.
All may be right… or wrong.
Have faith in what's *beyond*!

To my husband

What it takes many, maybe lifetimes, what others seldom find,
It took him minutes to acknowledge and relate to his mind.
When others count on thoughts to tell them, to help them find the clue,
He heard her voice, saw her reflection, touched her hand… and he knew.

He could distinguish in her features such substance and such depth,
As analyzing won't discover, regardless of time spent.
He recognized and felt inside him the filling of a hole,
For in her eyes, he saw her kindness, and pieces of her soul.

And you may wonder, as do many: can love happen so fast?
Intense connection of a moment—can that be meant to last?
How can it be that he found beauty where other people won't?
By having welcomed what most fear, and seeing what most don't;

By understanding, in an instance, beyond thought—knowing!—how
All love and life and all that's real can only exist *now*;
By deeply feeling, in his being, surpassing time and norm
That *love* is to perceive one's spirit, shining out through their form.

My great man

To my husband

I felt alone forever, and always prayed for you,
Through endless tears and fears I'd gotten so used to.
So overwhelmed by suffering, I learned so well to cope
That my eyes saw illusions and my heart drained of hope.

Looking back at my journey, I wish I didn't wait;
I wish I dropped excuses; I wish I had more faith.
And now, a little later, emotionally free,
Wish you met someone better than who I used to be.

I didn't think, at that point, I simply couldn't see
That happiness could happen, or at least, not to me.
I couldn't fathom marriage, children, a life of bliss…
You've changed my life, my vision, and gave me all I've missed.

You didn't need assurance to instantly give trust
And turned, in a short period, my sorrows into dust.
You've showered me with kindness and taught me how to share;
I love you more each second! You're my life and my air!

You've given me a family, new energy, new life,
Made me a happy woman, best friend, mother and wife.
You've gained and have forever, for always and in whole
My heart, my mind, my body, and each piece of my soul.

Thank you for being here! Thank you for being mine!
Thank you for being patient and for making me shine!
I pray to God to give me the wisdom so I can
Fulfill you every second, my husband, my *great* man!

Grateful and blessed

As I sit down in stillness, observing her breath,
Holding her little hands, as I pray for our health,
Blessed that she calls me "mom", blessed that he calls me "wife",
I am grateful it's quiet and peaceful, our life.

I am grateful to dwell within me and cause space;
For the freedom to choose, for the gift of God's grace;
For the practice of presence, awareness, the Now;
For attempting my best when I didn't know how;

For experiencing faith and for feeling the ground;
For the healing of time and vibration of sound;
For the joy to just be, hear the voice of my thoughts;
For observing the trends and connecting the dots.

I am grateful for learning and growing each day;
For the challenge and puzzle God put in my way;
For exploring my heart and for calming my mind;
For the goodness of life and a world that is kind.

I am grateful to learn to let go of my pain,
Leave what's not meant to be, what I wanted in vain,
Treasure what is for me, know there's sense in it all,
And distinguish what's mine from what isn't my call.

For the music, the cello, the spring, the fresh air,
The connections and friendships with whom life I share;
For the privilege of knowledge, the beauty of art;
For what brings me to tears and captures my heart;

For the wisdom of God and His grand, perfect plan;
For the wonderful gifts that He's given to man;
For He's taught me to love, put my fears at rest;
For all this and much more, I am grateful and blessed!

www.ingramcontent.com/pod-product-compliance
Lightning Source LLC
Chambersburg PA
CBHW031314060726
47590CB00003B/1216